Inspire Me Series
Book 1 & 2

Raw, Perception,

and

Awakening Dreams

Published by:
Poetic Resurrection and Sonia Iris Lozada
PoeticResurrection.com

Dedication

Mom and Dad

Thank you for your love and support.

Puerto Rico

My proud heritage.

And

All my family and friends for their beautiful and loving support.

I am humbled and grateful to you.

Inspire Me: Raw

Sonia Iris Lozada

Re-edited by

Ruben Rodriguez

Originally edited by

Brenda Varda

Spanish Language Editor

Maria Cuevas

Table of Contents

Introduction to Inspire Me: Raw

"Yesterday I was clever, so I wanted to change the world. Today I am wise, so I am changing myself." **Rumi**

Change is stimulating—It allows for new opportunities. I enjoy minor changes but having been thrust into an unexplored psyche after surgery, I felt the history I knew of myself dissipate. Losing my autonomy for two months is challenging, but the spiritual awakening that ensued altered those perceptions. The benefit from this event: I rediscovered my passion for poetry, a love from my childhood. Out of a lengthy hiatus these poems emerged: raw, uncensored, and full of what life emits.

This is my first published collection, which I release in hopes that my poetry helps others experience that they're not alone.

Introduction to Inspire Me: Perception

"A losing war is the one we have with ourselves."
Sonia Iris Lozada

Fear obstructs our journey in life, and by making peace with it, a new beginning of thoughts and actions follow. In the past, I believed difficulties in life were due to misconceived actions or a punishment from this or a past life, but now it's a motivator, telling me I need to change and perceive these situations as lessons, inspiring me to move and think differently.

In this collection, I've learned from life's moments of joy, fear, and love to accept with grace. My life today is so different from recent years. There's a sense of happiness and a longing for less material possessions: the joy of living without the burden of possessions. Clothing, furniture, and other items I couldn't prior live without seem so unimportant now. A true cleansing of life.

These poems were difficult to edit, because they dealt with obscure dreams, thoughts, and stories. The dreaming mind is left to interpretation. A frightening image to one is calming to another. I love wolves for their leadership and social behavior. They travel in packs—their family unit—but others have a contrary perspective.

This collection of poems and a story was meant for you the reader to travel life's journey with me

Sending love, joy, and blessings,

Sonia

Introduction to Inspire Me: Awakening Dreams

"In life there are pivoting moments of awakening."
Sonia Iris Lozada

The forthcoming book Inspire Me: Awakening Dreams has taken more time to complete than I had originally planned. Instead of the influx of poetry I normally have I kept seeing quotes and short stories. Ideas for talks which I use on my Poetic Resurrection Podcast. This book has much of what I felt we as a society and myself were experience. Yes, the pandemic has been challenging. I reflected much during these pandemic years and saw how much we need change. I needed to change. Awakening Dreams section is a paradigm of the times.

Enjoy! Many blessings.

Sonia

Citizen

Curly red hair
Freckled skin
Speaking Spanish
Not fitting in

People's biases
Perceptions
Ignorance
—Citizen

Where are you from?
How did you get here?
Was it a struggle?
No—Citizen

No boats
No tunnels
No hiding
Airplanes

I belong here
Born here
Educated
—Citizen

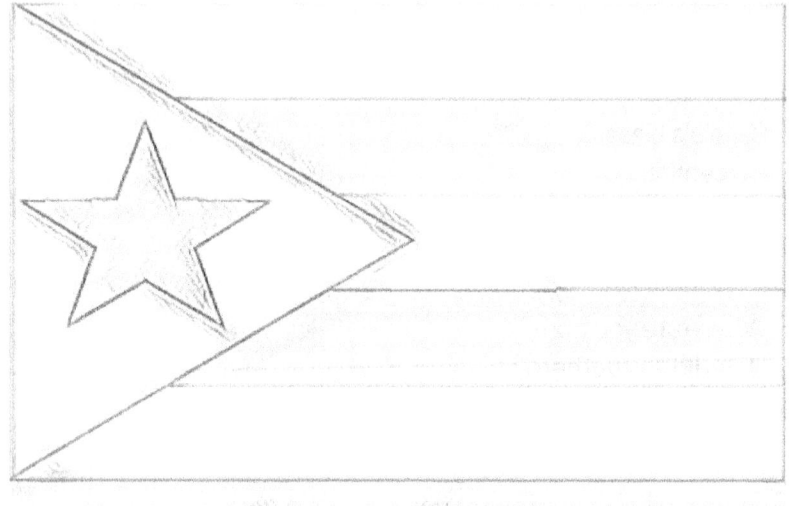

Puerto Rico

Ciudadana

Pelo rojo rizado
Piel pecosa
Hablando español
Sin encajar

Prejuicios de la gente
Percepciones
Ignorancia
Ciudadana

¿De dónde eres?
¿Cómo llegaste aquí?
¿Fue una lucha?
No–Ciudadana

Sin barcos
Sin túneles
Sin esconderse
Aviones

Pertenezco aquí
Nacida aquí
Educada
Ciudadana

Inspire Me

Inspire me—
Question, or plea?
Don't know
Don't understand

After so many years
Still asking—Inspire me
What to look for?
What do I need?
Asking too much?
Not enough?

Thoughts race
Anxious hands trying
To catch life's water
Slipping through fingers

What to do?
Where to go?
Trying to amputate
Claw from heart

Breath is shallow
Heavy weighted chest
Screaming but
Muffled silence

Does anyone hear?
Inspire me

Open to receive
Willing to change
Yet the claw clamps
Release me

Blessedness
Life shifts
Relinquish the battle
Purpose thrives

Inspired me

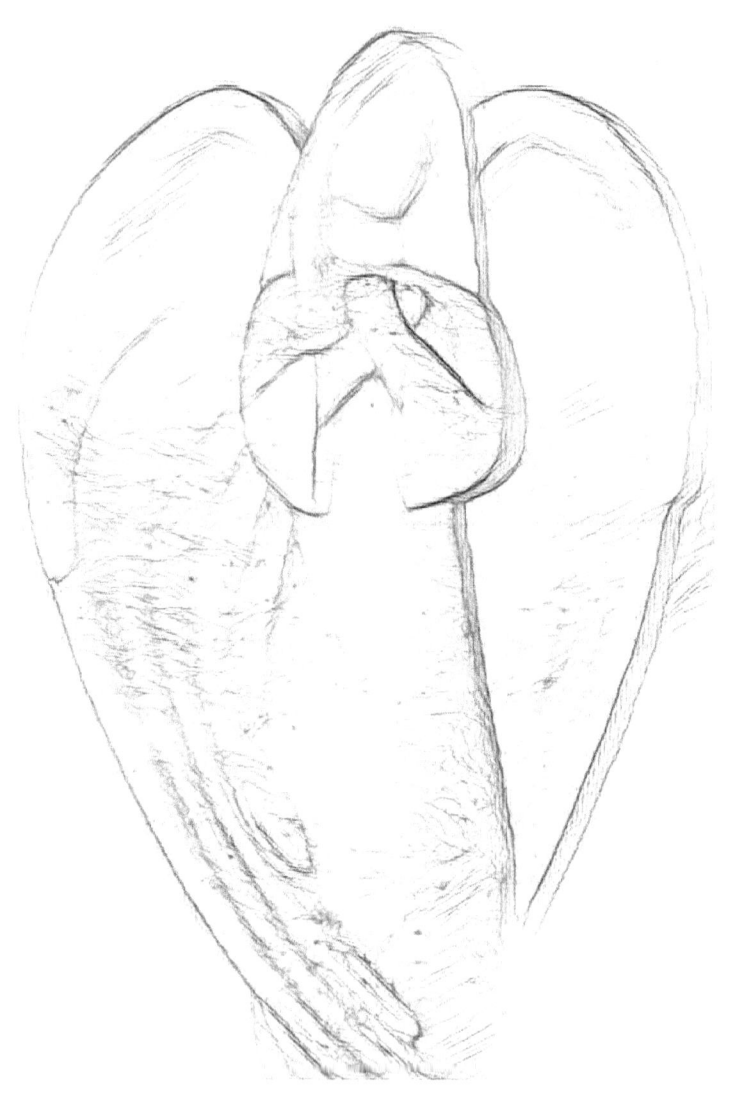

14

Angels of Earth

A girl cries on a park bench amid an
Unpierceable forest of mankind
An angel emerges to wipe her tears
A warm, secure smile

The angel flies towards heavens above
Tears in her eyes, and so God wipes them
An angel's wedged between Heaven and Earth
Not belonging to either—yet both

Afraid of not making a difference
Nurturing and protecting those below
At times crying out for help
Still giving without regrets—yet afraid

We're grateful for those fighting for our rights
Cherish those who protect the animals
Feel compassion for those who protect the planet
Enhancing lives—Thank you, Angel of Earth

Backspace

New page,
blank, blank, and blank
Tap, tap, tap.
Backspace

Writer's block, or
Have I exposed too
Much of myself?
Backspace

Do I want others to know
My deep emotions and vulnerabilities?
Backspace

My heart bleeds, but
I hide from all, not wanting to reveal
Feelings to them
Backspace

They have problems
They have pains
Don't want to add more
Backspace

Backspace on regrets
Backspace on hurts
Backspace on guilt
Move on—space bar

And then Mom calls

Child on a diet—teenage years
"Cabbage Soup Diet"
Lose five in three days. Great!
Cabbage, chicken stock, onions, and spices

Three days, no protein—too long
Shaking like wind against a fruit tree
Not a meat eater. Beans tasty
Make my soup. Turned out good

Large bowl—next day
Two pounds less. Yeah!
Bloated, but it's cabbage
Stomach agitates like an old washer

Stuck out there—excruciating gas
Holding a can of air-freshener
Spray, spray, and spray some more
Sounds like a balloon losing air

Mom's radar knows when to call
"Sonia, como esta?" Pain!
"Yo no sé porque tú siempre está a dieta,
Tú te ve bien."

Need to lose weight—camera adds pounds
"Yo no se porque. Gente en la televisión son feo,
y tú no eres fea."
"They're character actors, mom."

Need not be pretty. Tummy hurts
"Que te pasa, tiene Mal de Peo."
"Yes, farts.
I gotta go. ¡Bendición!"

"Que dios te bendiga
y que te traga suerte."
"Thanks, mom—love you."
"Love you too. Bye."

Earth cries for

Change of life

Cocoon

Last night a dream shook my soul
Simplicity at its beginning
An audition for singing songs
Lyrics of a different tongue—music was reggae
But why an unknown language?

My rhythm and vocal tone were enjoyed
Casting states, "Meet me at downtown club"
Scattered trash along the street
Submarine gray tattered building
Gothic facade—house phone, but no answer

A naive woman approaches
But sees this man's club closed—turns away
Bouncer approaches telling me to leave
Bird of prey grasp, escorting me out
        "Not a place for you, go home!"

Now—comfort oasis of home
Stillness in air and doom feels close
Happy song plays from phone
Director— "Where did you go?"
Handprint on arm—no more!

Noise outside door, the gargoyles fly
No longer perched on Notre Dame
These medieval protectors rise
Earth cries for change of life, for gargoyles aid
Brave wings expand across stressed skies

Frozen, unable to move—a concealed room
Faint in a cocoon of scaled wings
Embrace me—shelter
Figure changed—no longer frightened
Realize the captive wings are mine

Forget

Sometimes I can't remember: often, actually
The times I run out and say nothing to you
The times I am angry and pretending to be okay
The times I don't come home at night

Sometimes I can't remember: often, actually
When your anger lashes out at me
When you drink too often and hurt me
When you disappear into an aberrant abyss of time

Sometimes I do remember: often, actually
Your cruel words that hurt
Your desire to touch that repulses
Your anger at who you've become

I remember and choose to forget
Do you love? As those you love are hurt
Do you know the emergency room—a
second home?
Do you understand—Inner scars show more
than the ones I wear?

Sometimes I can't remember: often, actually
The raising of happy children here
The life we thought was possible
The comfort of a safe, loving home

Sometimes I can't remember: often, actually
How reality needs exposure

How I've always remembered
How lights slowly dim on you

Olvidé

A veces no puedo recordar, a menudo realmente
Las veces que me fui y no te dije nada
Las veces que estaba enojada y fingía estar bien
Las veces que no llegué a casa por la noche

A veces no puedo recordar, a menudo realmente
Cuando tu cólera me ataca
Cuando bebiste demasiado y me lastimaste
Cuando desapareciste en un aberrante abismo de tiempo

A veces recuerdo, a menudo realmente
Tus palabras crueles que dolían
Tu deseo de tocar que repulsa
Tu enojo con quien te has convertido

Recuerdo y elijo olvidar
¿Amas? Como los que amas están heridos
¿Conoce la sala de emergencias—una segunda casa?
¿Entiendes—Las cicatrices interiores muestran más que las
que llevo?

A veces no puedo recordar, a menudo realmente
La crianza de niños felices aquí
La vida que pensamos era posible
La comodidad de un hogar seguro y amoroso

A veces no puedo recordar, a menudo realmente
Cómo—la realidad necesita exposición
Cómo—siempre he recordado
Cómo—las luces se oscurecen lentamente en ti

My Solace in Paradise

Free Me

Tree swirls in the wind
Releasing fruit
Freeing birds' souls
Branches dance in light

My solace in paradise
Fancying a thriving life
Skylight warmth encases
Sheltered in a white chamber

A sparrow flies
Spreading wings, so inviting
Enticing and impressive
Lyrical messages soar

Engulfed in peace and comfort
Sprouting new light
Freeing tree of old souls
Liberating us

A rebirth exchange pact
Made from the beginning
Contract fulfilled
Immortal? No. Yet bliss awaits

Frozen

Sitting on a stoop in a barrio of Chicago
Summertime and everyone's outside
Escaping sweltering heat from
Un-air-conditioned apartments

Everyone vocalizes in Spanish accents
Puerto Rican, Mexican—some Gypsies too
It's Bucktown in the sixties

No attention to their surroundings
Cars breezing by—open windows
Giving relief to drivers

A two-year-old
Trotting down the sidewalk—Mom unaware

He steps out onto the street
Pounding heart—can't speak!

I see, but no words
Feel guilty, but can't move
He walks and hits side of moving car
Is thrown into the gutter
His mom screams, but he's okay
Life continues. Reliving that moment…

I did nothing. I froze.

Cold that Day

Consoling you is out of means
Hints I've left, dismissed
Ringing phone, please hear me
Voicemail—Talk to me

Loving you, leaving you
My heart weakens—I still love you
I wish you can hear the rings
I sense your tears, wanting to hold you

So cold that day, my bones trembling
Tears flowed to ice—then it stopped
Whisper of love, wanting to hold you
Now I can't embrace you—time hastens

The light Is bright as the path beckons
Family awaits—life abandoned us
I leave my life like
A peaceful flower on a grave

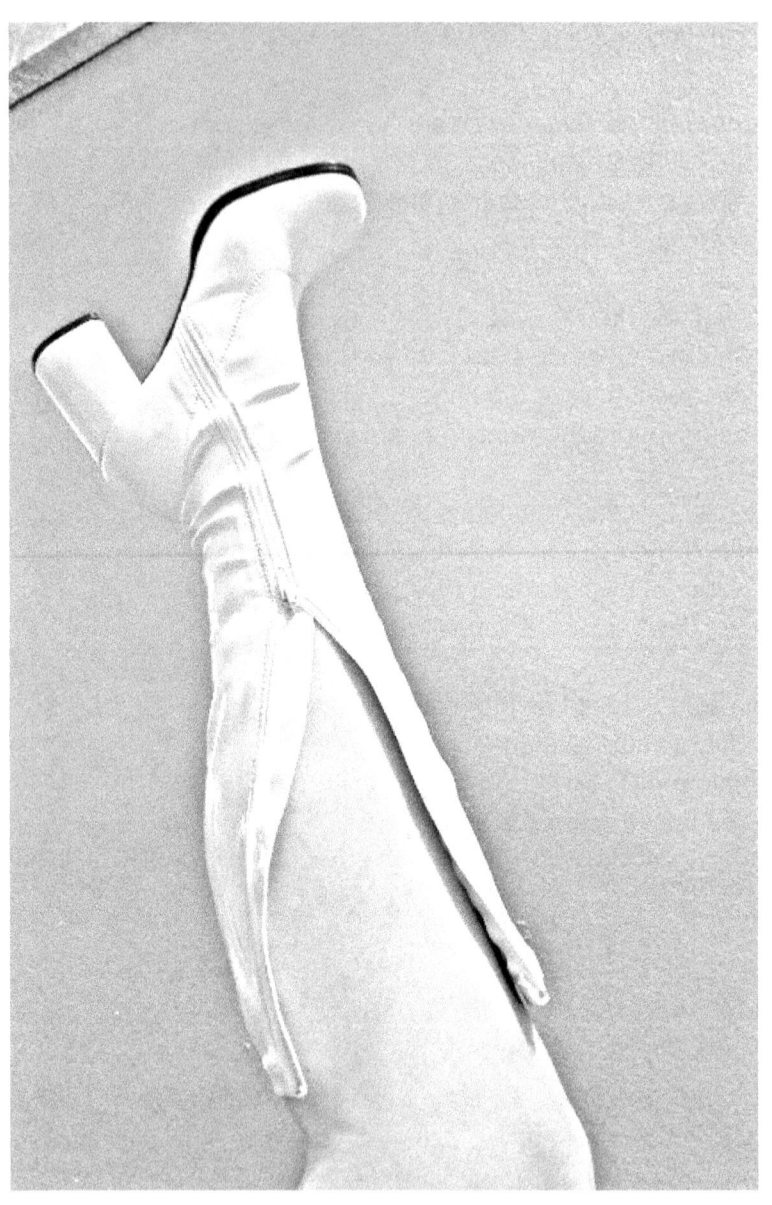

Go-Go Boots

At 10
Made a mistake
Told my teacher that I
Want to lose weight

First diet included
Liver, once a week—Yuk!
Different recipes, so nasty
That's not what I was seeking

Stood in line for free lunch
Menu: peanut butter cookies
My favorite munchies
I wanted one—Damn!

"Hide one for me, please"
When teacher's not looking
Don't want to get teased for
Failing program on first day

My mom states, "You're only ten!
No reason for a diet"
Wanting to be model thin
Groovy clothes—Buy them
Go-Go boots the stylish trend

Chubby clothes too short
Regular pants too long
Big kid bell bottoms reach calves
Average size bells at ankles

Others smoke bongs
Skunk weed smell
Permeates halls
Hide don't tell—jail fate in '68

What to do with weight
Insecurities begin
Entire life, same shit—wasted time
And now I'm fine

Joy

A gentle smile peeks through
An aged facade
A smile that melts my heart and soul
Carrying me three trimesters

Holds me tight when I cry
Loving by my side
So safe to have you here
So warm to have you near

       Alone am I? Not the truth
       Your gentleness, embrace, and love
       A blossoming flower of joy
       Blessing me from birth

Your gentle caring smile peeks through
An aged facade

Lilac City

Nestled near rocky foothills
Birthplace of Father's Day
Haven of outdoor adventures
Wealth of family life

Land of beauty: Spokane
Home to assassins—Why?
A father celebrated in
A haze of video clips

Rivers and lakes nourish
Tech life blossoms
Wildlife preserves while
Suspicious deeds breed

Grim shadows, summer of '96
Scandalous women vanish
Gratified passenger—cash on mind
Forbidden lust—leisure and death

Newsprint stains my hands
Headlines rage through my veins
No one deserves
Permanent sleep by highways

Sex—a bullet to the head
Money barter for her plight
White corvette red lights fade
Gratis prey—Is it?

Billboards on the road
Scream like a banshee
Life is Armageddon
In a peaceful family town

Siren—a daughter—police
Release without jail tonight
Decaying protein growing lilacs
Like in family window box

Gauzy thoughts prevail
Thirteen murders wrapped Yates's neck
Confined in *Place of Many Waters*
Near a town called Spokane

Meditation

Meditation, a blessing and a curse
Homebound, surgical cuts on foot
Captive for twofold months
Time presses to engage the practice

Mantra probing of inner thoughts
Only exposed to silent bliss
Anxiety succumbing to OM
Deep breaths of life-force. Soothing—No

Heart races grasping the thoughts
Flowing through mind
Blood roars through veins
As I breathe, breathe, and breathe—OM

Past lives flash like a melody
Deep secrets of the psyche
Don't want to deal again, old friend
A contract to stay hidden
Why after all these masked years?

Enigmas of the intuitive child within
Precious one, not forgotten
Who blossoms out in stillness of light?
Admit the past and move to Nirvana

Hesitation as I waver to agree
Script in native tongue of shame
No longer will I hide

Embracing the child and speech

Meditate for acceptance
Meditate for life force
Meditation slaps me in the face
It's a blessing and no longer a curse

Meditación

La meditación es una bendición y una maldición
Confinad en casa—cortes quirúrgicos en el pie
Cautiva por dos meses
El tiempo presiona para emprender la práctica

Mantra sonden los pensamientos internos
Sólo expuesto a una dicha silenciosa
Ansiedad sub-venir al sonido de OM
Respiraciones profundas de fuerza vital. Calmante—no

Carrera del corazón capturando los pensamientos
Fluyendo a través de la mente
A medida que la sangre ruge a través de las venas
Mientras respiro, respiro y respiro—OM

Las vidas pasadas parpadean como una melodía
Profundos secretos de la psique
No quiero tratar de nuevo viejo amigo
Un contrato que permanece oculto
¿Por qué después de todos estos años enmascarados?

Enigmas del niño intuitivo interno
Preciosa que no se ha olvidado
Quién florece en la quietud de la luz
Admitir el pasado, pasar a Nirvana

El corazón vacila con los pensamientos
Escrito en la lengua nativa de vergüenza
Ya no me esconderé

Abrazando a la niña y el lenguaje

Meditar para la aceptación
Meditar fuerza vital
La meditación me abofetea en la cara
Es una bendición y ya no es una maldición

The freedom

of a

Carousel

Merry-Go-Round

The freedom of a carousel
Excited by a horse ride at Riverview
A long-ago pleasure slips away
      Merry-go-round

Just like my past, it's now closed
Childhood memories I long to embrace
Protected behind steel gates and chains
      Of a vivid lifetime

Don't grow up too fast!
Parents advised
Run, play, and laugh
Maturity interfered
      Games changed

Hand-carved wooden horses
Painted red, blue, white, and gold
Others of assorted colors
      The ones I chose

Safety in innocence
Fun to be carefree
Living life with joy
      At the merry-go-round

Mom & Dad

Heroes—carried me at youth
"Let's go to the store," I say
        She walks to the kitchen
        Makes coffee and asks if I want some. "No, mom"
"Do you want coffee?" she asks again

Patience—It's now my turn
Strength she gave me

"Okay," she returns to her coffee

I keep it simple
Don't want to confuse
Don't want to upset
The impatience is me
My pillar of strength changed

I wish I could give her the world—her memory
        Dad still has his wit
        Same building—different units
"In Chicago people die," he says
"I know. Murder capital of the U.S."

Years of intolerance
Took a toll on ninety-year-old frame
Fragile, thin physique
Not the man I knew

Watching him cook leg of lamb with potatoes

He loves potatoes and rice
He's the cook in the family

Gentle removal of pliable meat off bone
Added with care to the stew
A dark man who didn't speak English
Mistreated from long ago

The kindness of one teacher
Taught me to speak the language
Mom and dad knew compassion
Wishing I
Could make life easier

Mama y Papa

Héroes—me cargaron en me juventud
"Vamos a la tienda", digo
Ella camina a la cocina
Hace café y pregunta si quiero un poco. "No mamá"
¿Quieres café? pregunta de nuevo

Paciencia—ahora es mi turno
La fuerza que me dio
 "No mamá no café", son las 6 pm
"Está bien" ella vuelve a la suya

Lo mantengo simple
No quiero confundir
No quiero molestar
La impaciencia soy yo
Mi pilar de fuerza cambió

Ojalá pudiera darle el mundo, su memoria
Papá todavía tiene su ingenio,
El mismo edificio—no viven juntos
"En Chicago la gente muere."
Lo sé, capital de asesinatos de EE. UU

Años de intolerancia
Hicieron estragos en el marco de noventa años
Frágil fino delgado
No el hombre que conozco

Verlo cocinar la pierna de cordero con patatas

Le encantan las patatas y el arroz
Es el cocinero de la familia

Quitando suavemente la carne tierna del hueso
Añadiéndola al guiso con cuidado
Un hombre oscuro que no hablaba inglés
Maltratado desde hace mucho tiempo

La amabilidad de un maestro
Me enseñó a hablar el idioma
Entonces, otros serán amables
Pensamientos y deseo deseando
Podría hacer la vida más fácil para ti

Night Terrors

Waking up in terror
My nerves resonate
Feeling like a hammer
Hitting piano strings

My body trembles
Unbearable mood at three a.m.
Why do you visit me spirit?
You say nothing

Sharp knife dices through my head
Wake, but don't say why
Why do you pester me at three?
I'll hear you out in the morning

Stop violent intrusions
Can't help you if I'm not well
Disappear—I will listen
When the sun breaks

Place

Home—I pride myself
Its warmth, inviting, peaceful
My tranquility

Living room—spacious
It's calming and welcoming
Compelled to entertain

Bedroom—quiet space
Flourishing sanctuary
Trance captivation

Office—chaotic
Papers that file drawers overflow with
Technology too

My mind—the office
Filled with useless memories
Obsolete systems

Yet I still cling
Time and fear. Recollections
Relinquishing thoughts

Inner voices guide
Mantra's deafening echoes
Let go, let go—now!

Missed Opportunity

Seeing you from the corner of my eye
I shake from excitement and wonder
Who are you? Sable hair, gray eyes
What do they say?

You smile and I want to turn away
Smiling back, I relax
Walking a mystical path
On good earth space

Friends surround us both
A woman approaches
A kiss on cheek, sweet and taken
Turning away, I show respect

Oh, to nourish a soul
With harmonies of speech
Filling the cocoon of sound
Laughter and language flocking the canal

Turn back. Quiet now. The table—empty
It's being cleared—nothing spoken
Viewing a space of could-have-been
Silence echoes my essence

Sadness

Drizzle of tears on a mountain
Chisels the gorge
Smoothing the surface—starting anew

Flow of waves from full moon
Surrenders like a soldier near death
Nowhere, yet peace

Mourning former actions
An abundant essence yearned
Live the now—dismiss the rest

Soul's journey brings me home
Master task—letting go
Rewound thoughts confirm

Dissolve elusive dream
Purge past yet debris clings
Sun warmth coddles me

Time wasted. Was it?
Serene breeze expels fears
Life's resurrection

Same

Contemplating
Day after day
Wonders of fate

Searching for work
Organizing
Wondering what I'll do today

Decorating
Writing this
Not knowing the end

At this point in life
I thought I'd succeed
By this time:

A house, a car
Children, husband
Yet none of these

Strange thing—
Content
I think?

So much, so little
Overwhelmed
Organize
Decorate

Write
Stability?
Day after day
I do the same

Little Girl

The little girl walks to school
Tenements line gray streets
She does well in school
Her five-year-old stature
Shows resistance and strength

Drawings of prismatic colors
Joy and glee adorn her face
Hesitant to show teacher
Waiting for praise—Teacher questions
She understood but couldn't answer

Teacher screams at her
Points. To disappear into.
The sea of moveable desk
She gazes at her tattered shoes
Her friend speaks English, she does not

Colorless teacher was unkind
To the little girl
who only speaks Spanish
Tears flow down her face
She hides—the teasing kids

Goes home, keeps to herself
Pretends to be an actress
Living a world that wasn't her own
Only hearing voices of a different land
Citizens we are, but not considered the same

Pretending while so young to be okay
Her seven-year-old friend
Says she wants to play
A store basement, dark and clammy
Her friend gazes on while she screams
"It hurts! Why did you do this?"

A teenage boy
Took friend's innocence and
Now he's taken the little girl's
Her soul and worth
But she doesn't understand

The store owner saves her
Atop soaring stairs
Bold voice of disgust
Vibrates the crypt
Boy halts—He runs

She now rests at home
A peeling gray wood porch
Third floor view—sits on step
Sunless hallway
Looking at the sky so blue

Doesn't know how she got there
Mind's a haze of events
Discolored panties, hand-washed often
Advertise the status of her little life

The bandages trying to hold
The innocence lost. It's too late

Mom looks at her—
Turns away and cries
Did she do something wrong?
Sorry you're hurting and doesn't know what to do

I'm sorry, mom
Don't mean to make you cry
Don't mean to make you cry
Tears never came to me
The little girl who didn't understand

La Niña

La niña camina a la escuela
Casas de vecindad en calles grises,
Ella es buena estudiante
Su estatura de cinco años
Muestra resistencia y fuerza

Dibujos de colores prismicos
Alegría adorna su carita
Vacila para mostrarlos al maestro
Esperando un elogio - preguntas del maestro
Ella comprendió, pero no pudo contestar

El maestro le grita
Señala que desaparezca
En el mar de escritorios móviles
Ella mira sus zapatos andrajosos
Su amiga habla inglés, ella no

El profesor incoloro era poco amable
A la niña quien solo habla español
Lágrimas fluyen por su cara
Ella se esconde—los niños se burlan

Va a casa, se queda sola
Pretende ser actriz
Vivir un mundo que no era suyo
Sólo escuchando voces de una tierra diferente
Somos ciudadanos, pero no nos respetan igual

Tan joven fingiendo estar bien
Su amiga de siete años
Dijo que quería jugar
El sótano de una tienda, oscuro y pegajoso
Su amiga mira, mientras ella grita
"duele,". "¿Por qué hiciste esto?"

Un adolescente
Tomó la inocencia de su amiga y
Ahora se ha llevado de la niña, también
Su alma y su valor
Pero ella no entiende

El dueño de la tienda la salva,
Encima de escaleras altísimas
Voz audaz de disgusto
Vibra la cripta
El muchacho se detiene, corre

Ahora descansa en casa
Se descascará el portal de madera gris
Vista del tercer piso - sentarse en el escalón
Pasillo sin luz
Mirando el cielo tan azul

No sabe cómo llegó allí
La mente es una nube de acontecimientos
Pantis descoloridos, lavados a mano con frecuencia
Anuncian el estado de su pequeña vida

Las vendas que intentan sostener
La inocencia perdida. Es demasiado tarde

Mamá la mira y se aleja y llora.
¿Hice algo mal?
Siente que estás herida, no sabe qué hacer

Lo siento mamá
No quiero hacerte llorar
No quiero hacerte llorar
Nunca me vinieron lágrimas
La niña que no entendía

Time Passes

Sun caresses
Rosy hues
I flourish as the
Breeze prunes

Exposed and cleansed
Past stripped away
Layers erode
Float down

Chimes of time
Naked in the wind
Grasp reflections
Petals float

Rain overcomes
Only a fraction stays
A stem with leaves
One last rosehip drops

Peaceful in the dust
Awakening
Sun caresses—new sprout
Rebirth from past

Urban

Metropolis of

Voices near

and far

Train

Art deco train station; urban metropolis of
Voices near and far. People rushing life
Will they catch up? Will I?
Modern train—now steam engine

A modern woman, but now I'm not
Victorian bustle weighs heavy on my back
Whalebone corset crushes my ribs—light breaths
Wooden carved window—moving train

Apache girl mixes herbs—I am her
Braided long hair—fringed clothes
Naivety glances back at me
My vision returns to 1789

Train steams like a wet burning branch
Reaches a French blacksmith—I am him
Forging musket barrels—drowning sweat
Abolish Ancien Régime

Travel train and its lifetime tracks
Reincarnates my many souls
Touring through a continuum
Watercolors my destiny—
        On the train

Tree

Sitting on an amazing tree
Cool breeze cuts through clothes
Sun peaks through branches
Encompasses leg
      Gives me warmth

Sun embraces my journey
Instincts say leave
But the tree possesses me
Such beautiful spirit
      Disobeying gravity

Scars where limbs once stood
Pain and grief of losing part of you
Yet it perseveres
Thanking the sun for its warmth
      Breeze that cleanses it
      Earth for keeping it strong
      Life for its nutrients

Lessons instilled by nature
Hundreds of years, standing tall
Rapturous influence
For the air we breathe
      Beauty that shows mindfulness

I sit on an amazing tree

Unsettle

The mouse runs in circles
While the cat teases it
I'm both the cat and the mouse

Panic attack

Pace back and forth—going nowhere
      Same place—same view
      Same life—same me

Panic attack

Angry. Trapped
      Breathe, breathe
      No answers—Why?

Anger arises
      Hectic work
      Wrong choices—wrong plays

Panic attack

Think, lament—Breathe
Tears, shake—Breathe
Walk, move—Breathe

Panic attack

Vulnerable

Call upon angels for clarity
Are they listening?
Meditate, feeling the joy
That enchants the heart

Meditate, letting go
Bliss surrounds me
Chill flows through my spine
Inspiration finds me

Energy flows through my fingers
Onto a notebook page
Close eyes and let life be
Unafraid to be exposed

Allowing myself to be
Love and consideration
How can this be hostile?
Vulnerable exposition

Cold sharpness, head to toe
Release, remove my mask
Golden light surrounds
Fulfills my existence

Esperando

Encuentro que estoy esperando algo
Pero nunca entiendo lo que viene
El sol abraza las plantas en el desierto
Como mi alma llora

La vida que estaba aquí
Se seca con los pensamientos
La vida que puede, la vida que es
La vida que sucedió

Los dolores me cantan de juventud
Creciendo en las calles de azul
Zapatos negros satinados
Medias blancas manchadas

Iguana corrió con miedo
Sufriendo sin lágrimas
Ojos que no quieren cerrar
Pero no ven

Estoy en las cruces del camino
¿Por qué?
Mi idioma de colores no les sirve
En esta tierra

Y Luego Mamá Llama

Niña a dieta—años adolescentes
"Dieta de sopa de repollo"
Perder cinco en tres días. ¡Estupendo!
Repollo, caldo de pollo, cebolla y especias

Tres días sin proteína—demasiado tiempo
Tiembla como el viento en el árbol
No como carne, frijoles sabrosos
Hago mi sopa. Resultó buena

Tazón grande—día siguiente
Dos libras menos. ¡¡¡Sí!!!
Hinchada, pero es repollo
El estómago se agita como una lavadora vieja

Atascada a un gas insoportable
Sostén una lata de ambientador
Rocíe, rocíe y rocíe un poco más
Suena como un globo perdiendo aire

El radar de mamá sabe cuándo llamar
"Sonia como esta?" ¡Dolor!
"Yo no sé porque tú siempre estas a dieta
Tú te ves bien"

Necesidad de perder libras, la cámara añade peso
Yo no sé porque, gente en la televisión son feos,
y tú no eres fea "
Son actores de carácter, mamá

No necesita ser bonitas. Dolor de estómago
"Que te pasa, tienes Mal de Peo"
Sí, peos
Me tengo que ir. ¡Bendición!

Dios te bendiga
y que te traga suerte "
Gracias mamá, te quiero
"Te quiero adiós"

Inspire Me: Perception

Sonia Iris Lozada

Re-edited by

Ruben Rodriguez

Originally edited by:

Eneida Maldonado

Foreword

I met Sonia Iris Lozada at a poetry reading not long ago. I was struck at that time not only by the imagery and color in her work but by the resilience, strength, and magic in her poems. It became important for me to know more of her poems and to follow where they would take her as the poet and me as a reader. Upon reading INSPIRE ME: PERCEPTION I see, in an even clearer sense, why these poems are important to me. I believe they will be important to you as well.

In this book, you will see poems that introduce you to the "Self" of Sonia Iris Lozada, and you will see an invitation to explore your own "Self," your own dreams and fascinations, your own regrets and hopes. In "Perception," you will be introduced to the prodding of dreams amidst caressing breezes and the reverence of the day's beginning.

Some of these poems enter the working world. "Just No" is a reminder of the disconnection and disillusionment that can whip our sensibilities to submission in the workplace, regardless of our own unhappiness and frustrations.

In "Continuum" the reader is pulled into the magic of the natural world, the way its mythology follows us into spring's lush loveliness.

As earthfall cleanses itself

Hope gathers irises

For a rainbow bridge

and with the voudoun magic supplicated from the earth itself

Oya conjures and flees the storm

Yemaya—mother—disappears

Amazon and Niger Rivers

Dominated

Femininity protected

Herein you will experience an everydayness so relatable you'll believe the poet pulled the images from your own mind. "Food" sits in our consciousness and manifests itself in the memories that so many of us have of home, kitchen, and family. The memory of love bestowed by a mother in a kiss on the forehead embraces us in "Warm."

In "Adaptations," Lozada reminds us of

stomach knotted

Breathe in–hold

Chest is tight

all the familiar symptoms of anxiety are as real and as complex as nature itself. *Nature's focus*, she tells us, *is asymmetrical / Disregarding self*

The collection closes with the poem, "Quiet." She ponders questions and seeks answers from *another realm / Beyond our three dimensions*, and, as the day darkens, she bids us goodnight with these words:

REM creating memories of

Longevity with peaceful

Nightfall sleep

Sonia Iris Lozada has given us through these poems an assurance of the way life goes on—with us, despite us. Well done, poet!

Martina Reisz Newberry

Author of: Learning by Role

Lost in Cosmos of Beliefs

Self

Perplexing stillness
Lost in cosmos of beliefs
Concepts—Old movies flash

Abstract intentions
The past is past—Face it
Embark to unveil behavior

Evolving blossoms
Efflorescing history
Conjuring spells of soul

Cubical cage of
Anxiety soars
Halts transformation

Conflicted thoughts
Tension of Id and Ego
No more, no more

Reticent shrieks
Guidepost confusions
Deceit impacts meditations

Metaphysics
Vanishing sage
Contemplation finale

Old beliefs release soul
Heart opens, engages
A benevolent self

A

Lonely

Soul

Alone

Sitting on a solid branch
There's clarity and confusion, just staring out
No movement in the muddled
Beauty of branches and options

Perceiving thoughts of entangled leaves
Do I proceed into the unknown?
Can there be escape, once entered?
What's there?

The mind tangles the web of life for us
Clarity holds thin branches, which
Negates the weight of experiences
Therefore, I sit still—frozen

Loneliness, chirping for attention
No sounds, utterances, or voices
Ignored
Then movement

A lonely soul approaches
Understanding the perched cry
Holding strong on the solid branch
I'm heard—My companion approaches

Kind eyes of sympathy
Warm white glow of self
Listened to anger of
Discontent and fear

Flying away

Above the tree of misperceptions
Where it's all clear
Where the heart breathes

Curiosity

Peeks outside

The Season

Crackling fireplace sings
Curiosity peeks outside
Autumn leaves
Hills of amber foliage

Chlorophyll vanishes into
Childhood joys and
Jump to the sounds of
Crushing maple leaves

Listening to music
Family reminisces
Not relating
I smile at my friend

Brother and sister join me
Hopes, dreams, and truths
Strange how we review life
Expecting more, regretting less

Winter possesses fall colors
Morphing into cleansing snow
Homebound readings of knowledge
House parties, holidays, and family

Fireplace logs disintegrate
Phoenix flames anew
Wood window frames
The still-urban terrain

Perception

Poetic dream speaks in verse
Melancholy tones—Guidance?
Joyful apprentice
Sentient sensitivities

What is it? Vital to aspire again
Dreams prodding
A breeze caresses—meadow
Soothing grass—sleepy dance

Awaken—nature's hypnotic rhythm
Performs—sharing air
Bliss and scent calms
Muscles surrender—sun on face

Glance within
Life's engaging gift
Courage starts
The reverent day

Eyes open to its embrace
Day's teachings prevail
Take deep breaths towards path
Grateful for this day

Just No

Talent manager sends contract in the middle of the day. Attorney reviews, "Was this a mistake? Red marks change proposal of what is not agreed. Managers indignant, rebuttal seized. Information sent via today's disconnected way—email. Worked with representative before now—Just no. Heartbroken, feeling like I can't get across a threshold from survival to thrive. No courtesy call to ease the pain, no inquiries, no answers to my questions. Just no. Don't understand—no time to squander, no time to waste. Just no. Disappointed by response. Disillusioned by alienation. Hurt—yes, just no. Why, I ask? No answer. Can we discuss? —No answer. Are you a friend—No answer. Just no.

Continuum

Spring florets glimmer
In afternoon light
Scent of fresh tulips
Myths of existence
—Fables

Trembling in 90 degrees
Veneer of tears
Illusions of turmoil
Created by self
Head spins—Pandora's Box

Seven sins tap across the stage of
A cardinal songbird
As earthfall cleanses itself
Hope gathers irises
For a rainbow bridge

Oyá* conjures and flees the storm
Yemaya*—mother—disapproves
Amazon and Niger Rivers
Dominated
Femininity protected

Travel—Antipodes
Indian ocean with full moonlight
Glistens as the waves erupt
Hera's* vengeful heart
Aches from illegitimate family

Crumbled mirror of water
Tears cascade past seven years
Moisture blooms lilies of death
Phoenix's ashes resurrected
In endless evolution

- Oyá uses tornados as her weapon and raises dead armies to use as her warriors.[1]
- Yemaya is powerful orisha who's the mother of living things.
- Hera is Zeus wife best known for her jealousy of Zeus' other family

Verse eludes

My

Thoughts

Complete

Hands tense like a taut anchor
Fingers twist with anger
Verse eludes my thoughts
Simple vow to complete two poems
Edit. Emotion retained? Staring, vacant eyes

Words swivel in mind—nothing set down
Blinking cursor mocks completion
Another poem. Tempo of heartbeat sounds
Like an apologetic new musician
Whose notes vanish on a staff

Focus and concentration are at battle
Pros and cons, bullets grazing ideas
And nobody should, could, or would
Mind drifts as waves tease
The promise to complete

Me

Optimistic—Loving
Caring—Positive
Healthy—Me

Outline—Yes
True—Yes

Why struggle?
Why fail? Why ask?
When—Enough?

What does it take?
What can be done?

Read self help
Do the right thing
Meditate

Breathe—Exercise
Love—Give thanks!

Hopelessness
Emptiness
Heartache—Sadness

Where did it go wrong?
What's missing?
It will come—Accept
Give thanks
Morning and night

Optimistic
Loving—Caring
Positive—Healthy
Me

Unraveling Soul's Agenda

Open

Persistent images
Unraveling soul's agenda
A masked core
Sharing inner confidences

Boundless exposure
Cloaking shield hides
Burning theories
Clouded obscurity

Pathless characters
Residing in gray
Planting firm beliefs
Yet favors avoidance

Fearsome exposure
Circulating life's breath
Relives in an excavated life
Where harmony is incomplete

Vessels of transparency
Illness beckons for attention
Sleep peeks thoughts of truth
Awakening to clarity

Open to love and change
As the mystic waters
Retrieve with sunlight
Dawn's redemption

Raw

Writing poetry
Do I sing?
Do I cry?

Afraid
Unveiled
Raw

Chains of a
Clenched soul
Breaking free

Shiver and
It hugs the spine
Sing and cry

Here I stand
Disclosing self
Exposed and raw

Harmony

Appeasing sounds of music
Chirps of robins
Melodies of each
Distant silvery flute wafts
Waterfall soaks emotions

Calming piano harmonics
Melodies of bass and treble
Hammering strings
Natures notes etched in a staff
Above and beneath

Single notes tell the story
Mesh existence
Ambiguous ninth chords
Composition of a
Serene triumph

Food

Reminiscing
Food stories that my family tells
About behavior
Don't remember, age three or four

Learned to walk, learned to climb
Kitchen chair, telephone books
God forbid family would
Buy a step ladder to make my life easier

An old refrigerator (not old back then)
Lever—jump up and pull down
Sister wonders why fridge is ajar
Opens door—Surprise, it's me!

Sitting on a shelf eating an apple
She grabs me, fights to get fruit
Tug of war ensues
She wants a chewed apple?

Stomping away (I had such an attitude)
Fruit in hand—I won
Sister retells story as family laughs
I am offended by their laughter

Rope around stove, fridge
Padlock on pantry? Chocks for candy!
Where's the fruit?
Watch fire in stove—I love fireplaces
Upset, storm off to yellow vinyl 50's sofa
Jump up and slide back down

Jump up again and again
Oh well, I'll throw myself on floor

Crying because I'm a miffed child
Check to see if they're watching
Mom comes over and hugs me
Sit on the big vinyl sofa—Finally!

Alluring Spirit Leaves

Defeated in Ashes

Soldiers march to kill me
Defeated in ashes
Who once were ablaze
In a misty terrain

The glorious sun
Alluring spirit leaves
Confiscated to cigarette
Smoke sates my soul

Given to mankind, a profit made
Repose—white room
Assuming full moon intrudes
Through sterile windowsill

Another shallow sigh
Can't breathe—Can't move
Life passes, withering while a
Soft breeze caresses face

Soldiers who marched to kill me
Defeated in ashes
At home where I
Long to be

Warm

Loving smile
Warm embrace
Gentle forehead kiss
Singing me to sleep

Sad child
Needing safety
Warm drops cascade face
She wipes them

Years pass
Fragile in time
Wrinkled smile
Love's blank gazes

Destiny gifted you
Being loved, a blessing
Devotion everlasting
Ease in loving you, mom

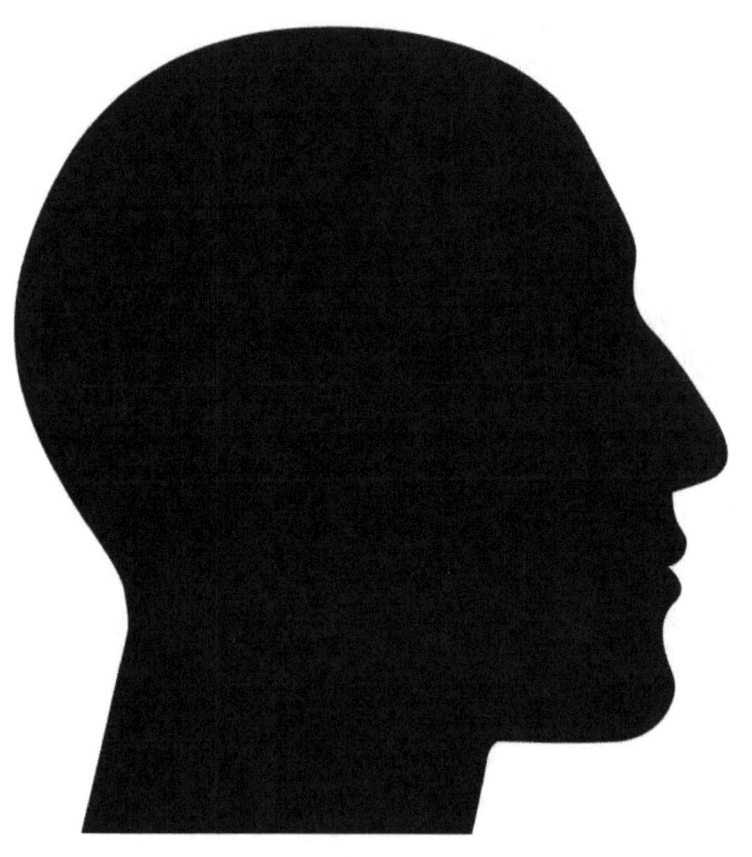

Silhouette

A dark shadow appears—soul shakes, the body
suspends. A story of an altered spirit who'll manifest
soon in the deepest of night. Shadow essence of two-
week visit encompasses my thoughts and sleep. *If
present, she'll be safe.* Who do you speak of, spirit? A
man's silhouette in the early morning as the streetlights
gleam upon glistening muscle tone. The sun peeks as
my roommate dreams, unconscious of his gaze. In the
darkness, a gun rises in his hand, aims at roommate's
head. Silence takes over as the smoke aura scars her
fate. Dream propels my slumber, and I go to her room.
If I'm present, she'll be safe repeats. Sunlight dances
on my face as the night's story whispers away. She
awakens, "Had that dream again, didn't you?" "Yes."
Three full moons calendar the sky. Gotham called for
her home—She's safe. Chitown childhood friends
summer evening visit—Sunset Strip. Summer heat,
sleep half nude as evening completes at midnight.
Vocal and joyful friends jest of a man at the window
where the drapes bellow. Amusement drains the night
as the muscles gleaming silhouette appears. She runs
into my bedroom, gun points at third eye—forced out of
comfort into the lifeless living room. Essence extends
my body as I guard the front door. "Think you're going
somewhere?" He shouts. Gun points for me to sit by
piano. The silent melody piano bench where I abide.
"On the floor," he casts me as he bares my skin from
sheet. Little sister weeps and window slams, fearing

discovery of his carnal acts. Guilt survival mission defuses the present. Escaping—leap two steps—first landing. Leap again, gun at head. Blinding movie screen of my life flashes, steals my sight. Land on corner of step and propelled onto the ground. *Not dying, not tonight!* Street or parking lot? A straight shot I will not be as I hide beside cars until I can jump a concrete fence that divides the building. Footsteps dissipate. Blood curdling screams echo in the distance. I climb many staircases and a man stands with two dogs. "Please call the police," I beg. "I think my friend's dead." His girlfriend's pink robe drapes a childhood fear. We hide. Police state, "Stay inside." Helicopter's beaming lights—Treble sirens and watchful dogs ease chaotic street. An hour-and-a-half, a knock. Police state, "He escaped—assaulted another woman and stole her car." Friends approach in a cloud of disbelief, sobbing. They heard my fall, calling—No answer—Saw my death in his hands. Police, "He'll return." Neighbor held us safe, and we slept on her floor. My scarred friends left the next day. Never went back. He never paid. Warning from silhouette, but I didn't understand. Premonition, and it's real impact. Checking doors and windows for a year, but I know I saved my friends because—**I was there.**

Children Play in Remembrance Forest

Forgiveness

Apprehension, love
Solicit approach
Many years, many times
Lacerate soul of past
Lost in gray storm

Sentiment severs green chakra
Dreams of refuge foretold
Waterspout of forfeited innocence
Adorn face like a well-read book
Agony lingers in cryptic mist

Children play in remembrance forest
Midnight stars intrude doubts
She cries in shame, alone
Forgiveness letters to child
Words scroll on page
Essence unfading presence
Caressing thoughts with joy
Messages of forgiveness
Desire warm embrace
Beatitude bestowed

Pissed

My Day

Alarm blasts me out of bed
Jump up quick, stumble on slippers
Purged into closet, hangers break
Upstairs neighbor stomps—Stop noise!—pissed

Like if unnecessary dive into clothes abyss
Wasn't enough, there's a complaint
Bite me, comes to mind
Falling was not on my to-do list

Coffee lid not screwed on right
Counter bathed in desired brew
Wipe quick before it seeps onto laminated floors
—Not waterproof—Pissed

Slow down, smell the roses
Sure! Now stuck with thorns
Alluring park meadows, morning walk
Sprinklers—Are you f**king kidding me?!

Bruised knees from ten-year-old desk
Continual hits and still don't LEARN
What does it take?!
Out of touch—Dense? Pissed

Watching TV, resting. Friday night
Smoke detector goes off
Pulled from wall, but it still rings
Get battery, plug back in—rings louder—Pissed

Going to bed early—use sleep aid

Stare at ugly popcorn ceiling
Building light beams on face
Cover face with pillow—Pissed

Alarm blasts me out of bed
Jumped up quick, didn't stumble
Hangers didn't break
Quiet and peaceful new day

Riddle

Beauty of rock formations
Uneven, unsteady, gravelly
Majestically standing tall
Moving with Earth's discretions

Fierce raindrops chisel away
Piercing winds soften edges
Sunlight burns, settles land
Steady foundation
Strong core and standing ground

Presence seen from distant land
Rolling visions mark my hand
Stand like a giant
Will not fall
Entertain one and all

What am I?

*Mountain

Online

Dating—apprehension
Online—embellish
Mature exterior
Thoughtful nature

Pictures gaze
Befriended at
Farmer's Café
Festive dialogues

Aloof presence
Wane conversations
Duet visions of
An absent man

Taming smile
Etched in memories
Fragmented myths
Remain

Adaptations

Stomach knotted
Breathe in—hold
Chest is tight
Movement—walk

Uneven pavement
Stare, proceed with caution
Thoughts of tasting concrete
Stumbling dance steps

Hollywood Hills
Unattainable dwellings
Violet hydrangeas adorn yards
Pistache trees—autumn shades

Yet nature's focus is symmetrical
Disregarding self—just a slight while
Purple sage smudges side streets
Sensations composed

How insignificant is anxiety?
Complexities of nature
Is so complacent—No battles
Just is—conceding to life

Spin

Spin
My outer shell
Clearing itself from daily life

Spin
Dirt, sweat, tears,
Joy, love, gratitude

Spin
Another day to recycle
Another day I'm clean

Spin
Fading with each turn
Searching deeper for truth

Spin
Smell of spring flowers
Smell of running water

Spin

Movement

Blue light leaps from TV
Mind's lethargic, yet alert
Remote—power off
Wired

Tossing like driftwood on a stormy night
Now mind races with daily thoughts
Hours later—elusive REM
Alarm resonates—It's morning

Dream's waves shifted to rest—too late
Heaviness of body clashes with daybreak
Three or four hours slept?
Synapses collapse and rebound

Café con Leche focuses verses on page
Nostalgia of parent's brew
Comfort, warmth, whisper haze of
Another day

Meditate, grateful for another chance
Chakra green light beams readiness
Mirror streams mist colors
Sheltered as morning glories blossom

Mellow

Doctor's office, 1976
"I want to get the skinny on weight"
Take one of these black pills every day
"Groovy." Just what I wanted.

So much energy!
Dance, play, and study
Sleep four to six hours
Go to class

Don't remember losing weight
Dancing every night
So bogarted two the next day
Big mistake!

Boogied over to my friend's pad
Heart feels like it's darting away
Not boogieing fast enough to catch up
Jive turkey—me

Sneak father's tequila, down shots
Didn't even get drunk—just mellow
Donovan's Mellow Yellow
                    Chillin'

Silence

Slumber eludes
Thoughts wander
Emptiness amplifies
Silence of a dark room

Mute path
Movements
Anguish
Silence

Vague answers
Remote viewing
Never there but here
Silence

Listen—nothing
Ponder—silence

Visions of dimensions
Audible light rays
Lost revelations in
Silence of a dark room

Dissipates

Observe dense forest of mind
Patient emissary—Wait
Smile. Walk the wandering path of
Life and sentiments

Weaved iron chest plate
Dissipates thread by thread
A plate worn for so long wherein
The green hue of soul hid

Going through life wearing armor hoping
To be hoisted on horse of dreams
Approach and you hold out your arms
Embracing as the green light beams

Struggle dissipates

Notes

Wind whispers at trees
Closing eyes that crave
Permanent darkness
Torment heart and bust

Wait for call
Lingering for weeks
Never reaching out
Hindered hold

Narratives echo
No contact, no concern
Neglect or fret?
Cracking vocal cords

Breath sings in 4/4
Plague of memories
Nature whispers at wind
Birds chirp

Plea to allies—encouragement
Disowning life
Relinquishing astral
Revolutionizing existence

Tomorrow

If I were to die tomorrow
Would I have organized my home
Would I have left my paperwork in order
Would I have made it easier for my family

If I were to die tomorrow
Would I have followed and completed my dreams
Would I have loved the way I wanted to love
Would I have visited the world like I wanted to

If I were to die tomorrow
Would I have told those that I loved that I love them
Would I have seen the beauty in my own life
Can I say that I lived my life to its fullest

If I were to die tomorrow
Would I have lived today
Would I have loved differently
Would I have felt my life was complete

If I would die tomorrow
A sadness would be there
To know I wasted so much time
Afraid of the unknown

If I were to die tomorrow
I would make the unknown

I'd face the unknown I was so afraid of
As I choose my life today with strength and joy

Purifying the Soul

Endless

Mind is blank
After many stories
All new ideas forced
Doing assignments
But all seem the same
Creativity of unspoken words

There's so much I want to write
So much I want to say
Mind is void
Poetic emotions
Purifying the soul—Wanting to cleanse itself
Is there virtue? Not at all—Awareness!

Days of contemplation
A peacefulness to this
Yet I go out in L.A. traffic and
Emotions go to hell
How could I meditate
And have such little patience?

Aren't I supposed to be calm?
Not in my case, obviously
It's an unacceptable reality
Optimistic yet malcontent?
Impatient with others
Is this my lesson to learn?
Bite my tongue and drive through L.A.

Journey

White path of nothingness
Emerald wooden door
Glass inlays brass knobs
Engaging luster

Counterpoint unclear
Juxtaposing meadow of silence
Forest speaks in whispers
No one's there

Look again—What do you see?
Crowd staring ahead
Why don't they see you?
Approaching to see what they see

Visit again—Do they see you?
Do they have open arms?
Are you wanted?
Do they care?

Yes, smile—content
Converging devotion
Embrace echoing oracles
Blind soul saw nothing until

The journey through the
Emerald door

Know

Chasing anger and have cornered it. A fearful, sad beast faces me as I approach and see terror in its eyes. I hold their hand and anger is calm. I'm sorry I enslaved you for so long. Holding you in my rigid heart. You were banging on the walls trying to escape, but I blamed you. I'm sorry. I thought you were hurting me, and yet you were just trying to escape. Trying to steer me in destiny's vision, to let me be, and I resisted. Lacking knowledge of your truths, and now I know. Here you stand before me afraid as the child who created you. Choking the past without comfort. I hold your hand and liberate you. My sorrow is great as life's whispers confess. I love you and let you go. Embracing you tight, releasing with love.

Thank you, fear

And Yet

Frustration impedes my thinking
Nudging distracting thoughts
And yes
I am frustrated

Knowing it's my perception
Others' issues out of my control
And yes
I am frustrated

Searching for employment
Months have passed—Nothing
Savings depleted
Job agencies don't listen

Online employment
Minimal responses
And yes
I am frustrated

Loving spiritual path
Yet live in a material world
Bills need to be paid
Residence maintained

And yes, I know it's me
Attaining responsibility
For passions and beliefs
And yet, I'm frustrated

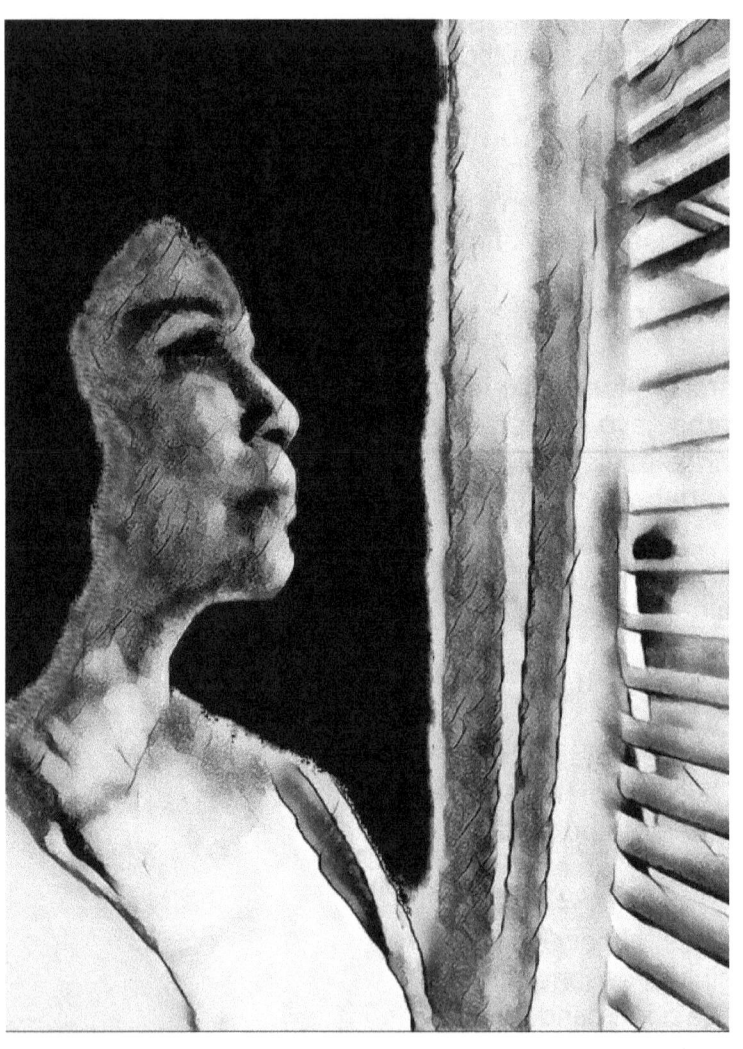

Quiet

Black and white
Chrome bedroom
Reflects silvery gray moods of
The uncharted mind

Incandescent garden lights
Shine through the blinds
Marking lines on face
Stares at the light

Answers from another realm
Beyond our three dimensions
Silence pries existence out of
Yearning questions

An essence enters
Smoky figure gazes
Into questioning eyes
Serene presence felt

Changing monochrome
Movie of thoughts and dreams
Reflect on cheeks and lips
Grin extends to essence

Crimson smile, blushing face
Sends joy to ashen figure as
Chromatic shades appear and

Smoky image disperses

Lights fade into darkness
REM creating memories of
Longevity with peaceful
Nightfall sleep

Good night

Inspire Me: Awakening Dreams

Sonia Iris Lozada

Edited by:

Ruben Rodriquez

Shade of Being

I stand on the beach, absorbing the indigo sky. The whispering breeze surrounds and envelops me as I breathe. It cools the soul. The waves creep up and work with the sand to mold my feet on earth. The Sun's desert colors—rays of light peak through the singing ocean waves, sounds of release and content. There I feel light, floating slowly over the water. I'm not afraid as I'm swept towards the light of eternal energy. The sea creatures do a singing infinity dance by my side. The sparkling eyes of these mammals transform my essence. I'm not alone. How long I have waited to go into the depths of the ocean where emotions ease life's pains as they bathe the skin in harmony. No entanglements, no reins holding me. I turn to see my past and see the shadows of my family and friends holding onto the remaining essence of the sand encasing my life, my experience, the memorable existence of each footstep we walked together.

Bound

Sorrow sweeps through my soul like
  The sword of yesteryear
Waves of sorrow smash upon my heart
Reminding me of you
  Of your love
  Of your kindness
I drown in the eventual stillness, gasping for air
Why was life so unfair to you?
  But it's me who doesn't let go
It's me who feels guilty for not
  suffering your loss longer
If I hold on to that feeling, then the memory
  Of you doesn't slip away
  Miss the feeling of our etheric touch
I dreamt of seeing your soul last night
  but I had tied a rope to it
  You kept trying to fly away
  But I kept pulling you back—You turned to me,
  broken
Today I cry and let you go—release you from the earth plane
  The rope unties and I see your smiling soul fade
  away

Alliance

Sometimes my essence aches because of the many adventures and events others have had without a mention, and I wasn't there. Is it me? Is the perception of what they sense I am determining my behavior, my thoughts? We spoke of holiday two summers long set for the third. The third visit around the sun and I asked when are we going? I don't know, was the answer. Facing the truth—via social media as I view the celebratory drink in hand with another. Visiting the places of visual beauty, of distant land we planned. Why not explain? Why falsehood? A sadness took over me. Was it them? Was it me? Was it my perceptions of childhood memories that stood in the way of the truth? A truth that hasn't existed in decades. A long ago feeling attached to a person whom I've surrendered my alliance. Taking responsibility for my emotions as I breathe and let go. Let go of my ideas of the past. Do I blame them? No, I'm accountable for my beliefs. Will we plan again No. Our characters detached the blinders I wore since childhood. Abandoning my memories and allowing myself permission to move on.

174

Memories

Today I go through my mom's memories
I go through her pictures
I go through her life's stories
I find her in the past
The memories she has forgotten
The ones from long ago
That linger in the glimpse of her life

Today I go through my mom's memories
The ones she has tucked away
The ones her strokes cheated from her
The painful memories erased
What can I do to make your life easier?
What can I say to erase your traumas?
Do I ignore—when you forget?
Do I keep your sadness in my heart?

Today I go through my mom's memories
The disappointments she kept close to her heart
The wanting to be loved yet feeling abandoned
The simple dreams she was deterred from
The disappointments fade
The abandonment fades
The sadness lingers

Today I go through my mom's memories
And merge my memories with hers
Feeling the sadness, the disappointments
Wishing the sadness to fade

I love you, mom

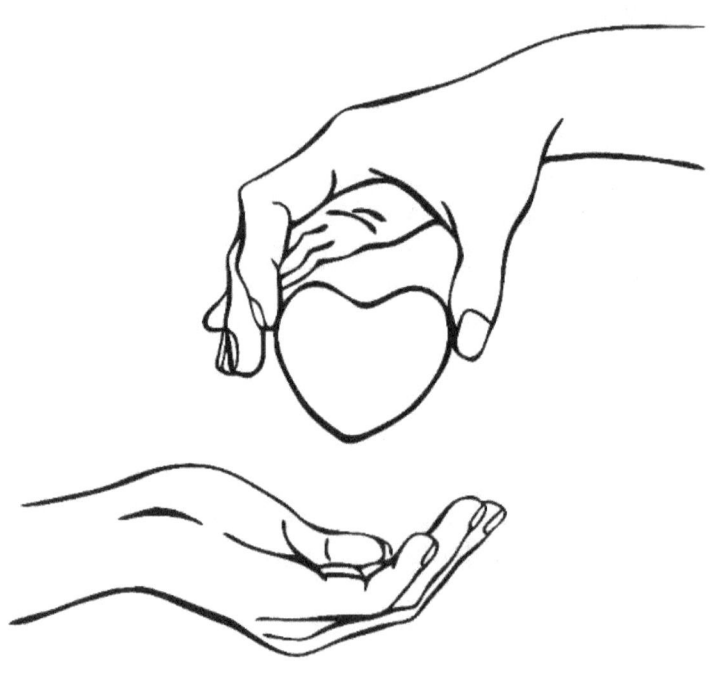

Love and Blessings

When thoughts
Overwhelm your being
Send love

When worrying about the family
And wanting to care for them
Send love

When sleep evades
When thoughts repeat
Send love

When finances diminish
And needs remain unmet
Send love

When feeling defeated
When feeling alone
Send love

When feeling fear
That life isn't fair
Send love

Sending love
Doesn't cost anything
Sending love
Brings us to the present

Sending love and blessings to you

Acknowledgments for Inspire Me: Raw

Writing this collection of poems was due to many wonderful people, and I'm grateful for their support.

Nancy Hinman: Thank you for inspiring me to write poetry again.

Martina Reisz Newberry: Thank you for your poetic insight.

Brenda Varda: Thank you for your knowledge, editing, and advise.

Maria Cuevas: Thanks, my Spanish savior and wonderful friend.

Mark A. Pearson: Thank you for your incredible advice.

Peter Konerko: Thanks for "About the Author" page and the original photo for "Forget."

Evelyn Eccard: Thanks for being a great sister who listened patiently through it all.

To my family, whom I love and appreciate.

Che Rae Adams: Thanks for your support, advice, and great friendship.

Tina Benez: Thank you for your beautiful notes and marvelous friendship.

Ana Urbina: Thanks for being there.

Gina Saucedo: Thank you, my spiritual friend.

Gina Amador: Thank you, friend.

Lucas Moen: Thank you for your support.

Thank you to everyone else who I might have missed. I have been truly blessed to have incredible people in my life.

Acknowledgements for Inspire Me: Perception

"At times, our own light goes out and is rekindled by a spark from another person. Each of us has cause to think with deep gratitude of those who have lighted the flame within us."

Albert Schweitzer

There are many people I want to thank in this installment of the INSPIRE ME series.

Martina Reisz Newberry for your great inspiration since we met. Thank you for your kind words and generosity. I am truly grateful.

I'd like to thank the following for their insights. I am grateful to (in alphabetical order)

- Che'Rae Adams
- Oceana Cato
- Crystal Giles
- Marlee Grant
- Nancy Ingram
- Chandra Jackson
- Camille Jenkins
- Lucas Moen

Evelyn Eccard for being a wonderful sister and for educating me in leadership.

Mark A. Pearson for going out of your way and always giving me the best advice.

Thank you for being there for me.

Thank you to all my family and friends. I'm grateful to have you in my life.

Sending much love and blessings to all.

Acknowledgements for
Inspire Me: Awakening Dreams

Thank you to all my teachers throughout the years. I am grateful and blessed.

About

Photo by Mark Attenbery

Sonia Iris Lozada is a poet, podcaster and performer fascinated with perceptions of time, history, dreams, psychology, and the metaphysical. Most of all, she is fascinated by interesting people, and it shows. Guests on her podcast, Poetic Resurrection, rave about her warmth, intelligent conversation, and genuine concern for what they have to say.

No doubt Sonia's success as an actor on both stage and screen, appearing in films such as *Out of the Wild* and *Expired,* play a role in her ability to entice guests to share what they know and feel with listeners. Described by casting directors as "a cross between Mae West and Rita Moreno," the Chicago native is the daughter of hard-working Puerto Rican parents. They were strong people who drilled lessons into her head: never lose your integrity, stay committed to your dreams, and always have a sense of humor about it.

Poetry has always been Sonia's way of explaining the bi-cultural world around her. The #1 Amazon bestselling author's publications include *Inspire Me: Raw* (2017), *Follow Akashic Dreaming Through* Time (2019), and *Inspire Me: Perception* (2019). Her upcoming book, the third in the "Inspire Me" series, is entitled *Inspire Me: In Time of Need*.

Her book *Follow: Akashic Dreaming Through Time* is currently being adapted for film.

Her Poetic Resurrection - Exploring Perceptions podcast launched in February 2021 with great acceptance. It is about the soul's journey and how our perceptions dictate our lives.

Further Reading

Other books by Sonia Iris Lozada

- ***Follow: Akashic Dreaming through Time***
- E-book and Paperback
- Available on Amazon
- ***Inspire Me: Awakening Dreams***
- E-book and Paperback coming soon.

Website: https://poeticresurrection.com/

Poetic Resurrection Podcast:
https://poeticresurrection.podbean.com/

Facebook: www.facebook.com/poetic.resurrection

Instagram: www.instagram.com/poeticsonia/

YouTube: https://www.youtube.com/poeticresurrection

Chica and the Man Podcast: A fun and light podcast.
https://chicaandman.com/cm-podcast/